The Wig

by Susan Hartley • illustrated by Anita DuFalla

Dan, Tam, and Gus are at the mat.
Dan has a red wig.
He has a hat on top of the wig.

Tam has a tan wig and a hat with a pin on it.
Can Dan win?
Can Tam win?

Gus has a wig.
The wig is a mop.
Tim can see the mop.
He bit the mop.

"My wig is wet.
I cannot win," said Gus.
Gus and Tim are sad.

Dan and Tam look at Gus.
Dan and Tam look at the wet wig.

"Here, Gus. You can have my red wig," Dan.
"Here is my hat," said Tam.

Can Gus win?